T11618

D1472225

G   ES

To my husband, D. J. Dougherty

Published by Willowisp Press
801 94th Avenue North, St. Petersburg, Florida 33702

Printed in the United States of America

4 6 8 10 9 7 5

ISBN 0-87406-661-1

Contents

Introduction 5

The Gray Man 9

The Haunted Highway 23

The Witch Hunter and the Curse 35

Messenger for a Ghostly Love 49

The Beauty and the Vampire 61

The Plantation Witch 77

The Haunting of the White House 89

Houdini's Return 99

A Weird Tale of the Wild West 109

The Rat Mummy 121

Introduction

Close your eyes and pretend you're traveling way back in time. Imagine what the world was like three hundred years ago. There are miles of thick forests, where tree leaves whisper and branches creak in the wind. Nestled in the hills are hidden valleys, dark and still as night. An overgrown dirt road leads to a solitary house with secret passageways and an attic full of mysteries.

In this world of long ago, it's easy to believe that a witch lives in the cottage by the clearing. It's easy to imagine a werewolf appearing in the light of the moon. It's easy to pretend that a ghost still resides in the rickety old house it lived in as a flesh-and-blood human being.

Close your eyes again and travel back to the present. Imagine you're standing on a city street corner. The world is a very different place from what it was three hundred years ago. The houses are built right next to one another. Apartment buildings loom tall and silent. Bright streetlights make roads, buildings, and lawns visible all night long. Telephones keep people in contact with one another; televisions keep lonely people company.

But look around you one more time and consider this: Even today, with the bright lights and super technology and the hustle and bustle of modern life, vampires are said to stalk their victims down deserted city streets. Witches may well cackle when it rains and rains and rains. Ghosts just might wander upstairs halls.

Yes, there are those who say that ghosts still haunt the living—and some people claim that they have actually seen ghosts or communicated directly with the spirits of the dead. Can these claims possibly be true? Did ghosts and haunted places exist three hundred years ago? Do ghosts and spirits make their presence known to us today?

The stories in this book will help you decide for yourself the answers to these questions. Here, for your spine-tingling entertainment and chilling excitement, are real-life accounts of strange occurrences and supernatural phenomena—events that logic cannot always explain. You'll find stories about witches and spirits, ghosts and vampires. Some stories are drawn from the past, others from the present. But at one time or another, each story has been believed to be true. And for some people, these stories are evidence that ghosts do in fact exist, that spirits really do return to earth from the spirit world, and that people actually communicate from beyond the grave.

You'll meet the ghost of one of America's greatest presidents, and you'll read about the spirits that return to reenact Custer's Last Stand. You'll learn about a vampire from long-ago Russia and a witch who was burned at the stake. You'll also witness a strange highway accident that occurs again and again, meet a woman who delivers a message from the great beyond, and discover a ghost who claims to be the spirit of the great magician Houdini himself.

So curl up on the sofa or on your bed. Sip a little bit of hot cocoa. And above all, get ready for some shivery fun!

The Gray Man

*Q*UICKSAND *is a sinister substance. Found on the bottom of streams and along seacoasts, quicksand is made up of tiny, smooth grains of sand drenched with water. These fine grains of sand don't stick to each other. Instead, they easily yield to any weight or pressure on the surface of the quicksand. If a person steps in the damp sand, he or she may be sucked under, sinking deeper and deeper into the muck. And the more a person struggles to get free, the easier it is to be pulled all the way under.*

Over the centuries, beds of quicksand have swallowed many secrets and many lives. Perhaps that is why stories of those who have been trapped by quicksand have

11

been told and retold through the years. "The Gray Man" is one such story. It is based on an incident that took place long ago on an island off the coast of South Carolina.

The stars glittered like diamonds in the night sky. The moon lit the shore. One after another the waves rolled in, hitting the quicksand with a sizzling roar.

No one was there to see the movement, the sand that shifted as the waves rolled back. No one saw the hand appear, reaching up out of the sand. No one saw the arm that followed the hand, or the shoulder that gradually surfaced from the muck.

And there was no one to see the head, bearded and glowing gray blue in the moonlight.

Slowly, the man emerged from the mire. The muck that covered him made him look gray from head to toe. Quicksand dripped from his beard, his hair, and his cap. In one hand he held an old-fashioned lantern, rusted and caked with dirt. The lantern cast a weak yellow light in the surrounding darkness.

The Gray Man looked out at the sea. He turned and looked at the land. Then he

roared with the waves.

"Beware!" he shouted. "Beware!"

And then, very slowly, he sank back into the quicksand beneath him. A wave rolled in, then another. The Gray Man had disappeared.

*   *   *   *   *

The mysterious Gray Man made his first appearance some 250 years ago, back when America was made up of colonies, not states.

In those far-off days, there lived a beautiful young woman who was in love with a handsome young man. The woman's name was Helena, and she lived on an island off the rocky Atlantic coast. Her lover, Richmond, lived on the mainland, in the South Carolina colony.

Whenever he sailed to the island on business, Richmond spent as much time with Helena as he could. And when they were together, they were so happy that they smiled and laughed from morning to night. They took long walks along the beach. They watched the great wooden ships come into the misty harbor. They watched the sea gulls flying overhead. They talked and talked, and one moonlit night they decided to get married.

Richmond could not have been happier. When he was ready to sail back to the mainland, he promised he would return quickly—and for good. He wanted to ask Helena's parents if he could marry their daughter. He planned to buy a cottage on the island where he and his new bride would live.

When Helena waved goodbye to Richmond, she did not cry. She knew she would see him again very soon and that from then on they would never be apart.

Helena waited eagerly for Richmond's return. She kept herself busy by baking bread and tending the small garden behind her parents' cottage. She cleaned the slippery fish her father caught in his well-worn net. She helped her mother salt the fish to keep it fresh. She darned stockings and she dried herbs for stew.

Above all, Helena waited. She tried to be patient, but it was difficult. She was too excited about her upcoming marriage.

Finally, the night Richmond was due back on the island arrived. Helena made a chocolate cake in the shape of a heart. She placed two tall, elegant candlesticks on the table. She put on her pretty blue dress and tied white roses into her thick brown hair.

Helena's parents smiled as they watched their daughter prepare for the young man's arrival. Not so long ago, they too had been young and very much in love.

But the night air was very foggy. There had been a storm earlier in the day, and the moon and stars were hidden by thick, dark clouds. The shore could barely be seen in the mist.

Fortunately, Richmond was a very good sailor. He steered his small fishing boat very carefully through the rough, swirling waters. He skillfully rode the waves and battled the currents. He never took his eyes off the angry water as his boat made its way to the island where Helena was waiting.

At last, the boat landed on the island's sandy beach. Richmond sighed with relief. He threw his anchor overboard and picked up the lantern near his wheel. He hopped off the boat and began to walk—or rather, he *tried* to walk.

With growing horror, Richmond became aware of what he could not have seen in the mist. His boat had landed near some slithery quicksand. His feet sank deep into the muck, then his legs.

Richmond tried to pull his body out of the quicksand. He thrashed his arms and kicked his feet, but it was no use. The quicksand kept pulling him under, swallowing him alive!

Soon Richmond's arms disappeared in the mire, then his neck, and finally his head. His hat skimmed the surface of the quicksand, bobbing up and down like a buoy in the water. Soon it too was gobbled up.

Richmond was seen no more.

At her family's cottage, Helena waited all night for Richmond, but he never appeared. Nor did he show up the following day, or the day after that. Helena refused to give up hope, but she was so sad that she cried all the time. She couldn't eat and she couldn't sleep. She took long walks on the beach, hoping to find a clue to Richmond's whereabouts. And all the time she prayed that Richmond would magically appear.

It was no use. As she walked the beach all she saw were piles of seashells, clumps of seaweed, and pieces of driftwood washed up by the tide.

One evening Helena walked the beach until long past sunset. It was a damp, misty night, much like the night Richard had disappeared.

As Helena approached the spot on the beach where her lover had perished, she saw a shape in the fog just a few feet ahead of her. As she came closer, she saw that the shape was a man—a man who was gray from head to toe as if he were covered in quicksand!

The Gray Man was holding a lantern. His free arm was extended straight out in front of him, as if he were pointing at Helena. It was as if he were trying to say something to her, trying to warn her.

"My love," the ocean seemed to whisper as it rolled in and out from shore, "be warned."

"Be warned, my love," the wind seemed to howl as it blew in from the sea. "Go away. Go away before the next night falls."

The Gray Man continued to reach out toward Helena, the lantern dangling from his quicksand-covered fingers.

Helena shuddered, then cried out. The Gray Man looked just like Richmond. He *was* Richmond.

"Beware!" the Gray Man groaned. This time Helena knew it was definitely not the ocean whispering. It was not the sound of the shuddering wind. It was Richmond, and he was speaking to her.

"My love!" Helena cried. She ran toward the spot where the Gray Man stood. But he had already vanished into the mist.

Helena picked up her skirts, turned, and fled home as fast as she could. She burst through the front door of her cottage and fell to the floor, crying inconsolably. Her parents tried to calm her, and finally they managed to put her to bed. Her mother brought her some tea, and her father put another quilt over her to keep her warm.

As Helena sipped her tea, she told her parents what had happened on the beach. But they didn't believe her. They thought she was hysterical. They told her to go to sleep and said that the next day they would take her to a doctor.

But Helena did not want to go to the doctor. Instead she begged her parents to take her to the mainland. "Just one day off the island," she pleaded. "Just one day and I promise I'll never mention the Gray Man ever again. Please!"

Her parents looked at each other. Their daughter was so insistent. Helena saw them weakening. She pushed on. "Mother, remember the imported linen you ordered? Maybe the store has gotten it in."

Helena's mother nodded. "Yes, that's true," she said.

"And Father," Helena continued, "haven't you been wanting to buy new gardening tools?"

Her father shrugged. "Yes, that is so."

Helena kept going. "And we haven't seen the Harrisons for such a long time, not since the last time we went to the mainland. I miss Marilyn so much. Oh, please, let's go!"

The last plea did it. "Enough!" Helena's father said. "Calm yourself, child. We will take the boat tomorrow and go to the mainland." After all, he thought, what is the harm in leaving the island for one day?

Reassured, Helena stopped crying and soon fell asleep.

The next morning, the family left the island in their boat. But while they were on the mainland that afternoon, an unexpected hurricane swept across the island. The storm was so strong and so sudden that it took everyone by surprise. Many people were killed and dozens of homes were destroyed. But Helena and her parents were saved—thanks to the Gray Man and his warning.

True to her promise, Helena never mentioned the Gray Man again. Yet she knew he was out there where the sea met the sand. She knew he would always be there, protecting her from harm.

* * * * *

Some say the Gray Man still walks the shore today. Some say he's looking for his lost love and waiting to help others wandering in the mist.

If you ever go to that island and walk the beach at night, take heed. Watch and listen. You just might see the Gray Man and hear him say, "Beware!"

He just might be talking to you.

The Haunted Highway

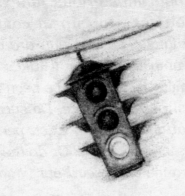

*O*LD, *abandoned houses. Dark, deserted forests. Rain-drenched, fog-covered streets. These are common settings for ghost stories. And when we're in such places in real life, we almost expect a ghost to pop out of a closet or grab at us from behind a tree. It wouldn't surprise us to see a monster walk out of the fog or hear a spirit moan an unearthly sound.*

Scary stories about places like these are very familiar to us. Indeed, such stories have become part of our culture, like stories about Santa Claus. Sometimes scary stories have value. They may offer an explanation of the creepy unknown. And sometimes they stop us from going full steam ahead into dangerous situations.

Stories about mysterious, unexplained events sometimes crop up in completely different locations. The tale you are about to read is an example. Although it takes place in California, similar incidents have been reported in the Midwest and elsewhere. Do such stories offer proof that ghosts really exist, persistently haunting the scene of death? Or do they simply show how strange and weird our imaginations can be?

You decide. . . .

———————
———————

He was a good driver, Mr. Johnson was. As his headlights swept past the thick forest on that cold, rainy night, he kept saying to himself over and over, "I'm a good driver and there's nothing to be afraid of."

There were no houses in sight, no people, not even a deer waiting to cross the road. Just trees, dark and threatening. Just rain, beating on his windshield. Just wind, blowing the storm clouds across the sky.

"I'm a good driver," Mr. Johnson repeated out loud. "And I can make it home just fine."

But there was no one to hear him. And

the storm was getting worse.

* * * * *

Only a few short hours ago, the sun was shining under bright blue skies. Mr. Johnson had finished a business meeting with a new client in San Diego. When the meeting was over, he shook hands with the client and walked out of the busy office building. Humming to himself, Mr. Johnson strolled over to his car in the parking lot. He got in his car, put on his seat belt, and looked all around for pedestrians before driving away. He was smiling. He was very pleased with the way the meeting had gone.

Mr. Johnson glanced at the clock on the dashboard. With a little luck, he would be home in time for supper.

The rain didn't start until four o'clock. The sky turned overcast with thick, steel-gray clouds. The wind picked up, swirling leaves across the road.

Soon the rain was coming down so hard that even with the windshield wipers at the highest speed, Mr. Johnson could barely see a thing. Lightning and thunder filled the skies. To make matters worse, a heavy fog was settling in.

Mr. Johnson eased up on the accelerator. He sat up very straight and gripped the steering wheel tightly. Even though he loved living way out in the California woods, driving in these terrible conditions made him wish he had never moved his family out of the city.

And then the worst happened. The highway Mr. Johnson always used was closed down because of flooding. He couldn't get on the entrance ramp.

"Darn!" Mr. Johnson said, hitting the steering wheel with his fist. There was nothing to do but continue along on the local roads and pray that the rain would soon let up and the fog would clear.

But the rain only came down harder and the pea-soup fog grew thicker. As night fell, the sky grew so dark that Mr. Johnson felt like he was driving through a cave. The wind rocked the car. The rain hammered down nonstop on the roof. Mr. Johnson was afraid he'd never get home. "I can do this," he mumbled to himself. But he wasn't really sure that he could.

Mr. Johnson slowed down even more.

Suddenly, through the rain-spattered windshield, he could see a red, watery glare.

As he got closer, he realized that the glare was a traffic light, strung up on wire across the highway. He came to a stop and looked around, trying to get his bearings.

The traffic light was bobbing in the wind. There were distinct white lines on the ground below it. Mr. Johnson had come to a crosswalk. Civilization! Maybe there was a motel nearby, or a diner where he could get a cup of coffee and wait out the storm.

The light turned green. Mr. Johnson began to drive slowly through the crosswalk when suddenly he saw a shape looming in the darkness in front of him. An old, hunched-over woman in a brown coat was standing in the middle of the crosswalk—right in front of his car!

The woman, her face shadowed and wrinkled in the glare of his car's headlights, turned and stared at him.

Mr. Johnson jammed his foot on the brake. "Look out!" he yelled. But it was too late to stop.

Then, at the moment of impact, he saw another car heading directly toward the woman from the opposite direction. Mr. Johnson shouted, "Oh, no!"

Headlights met in a glare of bright white light. Tires squealed. The cars swerved in opposite directions. Steam swirled up from the blacktop, mixing with the fog and the rain. The wind blew.

Mr. Johnson pushed open his car door. He jumped out of the car and ran over to the crosswalk.

The driver of the other car, a young woman in a raincoat, also ran over to the crosswalk. She was crying, "I hit her! I hit her!"

Mr. Johnson looked up. "No, no, I hit her!" he said. "It was my fault!"

They both looked down, terrified by what

they expected to see. But there was nothing on the ground. There was no blood, no body, no old woman. There was nothing there at all.

Mr. Johnson and the other driver stood in stunned silence.

Just then a police car, its siren wailing and its lights flashing, pulled up to the crosswalk. A policeman calmly got out of the car. "I would have gotten here sooner," he said, "but I just didn't think anybody would be driving around in this weather." He looked at his watch. "Yep, right on time," he said.

Mr. Johnson stared at him, his mouth open. "How can you just stand there like nothing happened? There's been a terrible acci—"

The policeman held up his hand. "There was no accident. At least not tonight," he said.

Mr. Johnson and the woman exchanged confused glances.

The policeman shook his head, then smiled grimly. "Let's sit in my car for a minute and get out of the rain," he said. "I have a strange story to tell."

As the rain poured down and the wind blew, the policeman talked. He explained that every year, at exactly this same time, at least one driver reports a car accident. "Just like you," he said, "these drivers claim they'd hit an old woman. Just like you, they found out they never did hit a soul."

"But," the policeman went on, "twenty years ago this evening, an old woman in a brown coat *had* been walking across the road. Two cars *had* been approaching in opposite directions. Neither driver saw the woman until it was too late."

Struck by both cars, the woman was killed instantly. And every year since then, at the exact same time of night, the old woman comes back to the crosswalk, reliving her last moments on earth. "Sometimes a car drives by, sometimes not," the policeman said. "But she's always there, standing right in the middle of the highway, rain or no rain."

The policeman looked intently at both his listeners. "Believe it or not," he said, "you have just seen a ghost."

Mr. Johnson was in shock. And he was very, very tired. He didn't want to think about what had happened. He wanted to go home. The policeman escorted him to the main highway, and forty-five minutes later Mr. Johnson parked the car in his driveway. He sighed with relief.

From then on, Mr. Johnson took the bus when he had to meet with his clients in San Diego. He never drove past that crosswalk again.

But sometimes, when he woke up in the middle of the night, Mr. Johnson would see that woman in the brown coat standing at the foot of his bed. She would be staring right at him, just as she did that night in the crosswalk. He would see her ghostly face, bruised and bloodied, break into a twisted smile.

The old woman would laugh and laugh, then disappear into the night.

The Witch Hunter
and the Curse

*B*ELIEF in witchcraft has a long history in North America, dating back to the early colonial days. In the late 1600s, a young girl named Sarah lived in Salem, Massachusetts. She and her friends began accusing others in the town of being witches. They claimed they saw their neighbors change into owls and bats. They swore that these witches cursed their fields and burned their houses.

The girls' accusations led to the Salem witch trials of 1692, which took place in a church. The accusers pointed their fingers at the people sitting in the pews. The accused knelt in tears on the stone-cold floor. The trials were a live drama, and onlookers jammed the church to watch.

Before the Salem witch trials were over, two hundred people had been accused of being witches. Nineteen people were executed for practicing witchcraft. And one man was pressed to death with stones because he refused to plead his innocence or guilt.

"The Witch Hunter and the Curse" takes place in a small town in what is now the state of Maine during the days of the witchcraft panic that spread throughout New England.

———

Dawn was just breaking. A rooster sang out and announced the day: *Cock-a-doodle-do!* A few birds chimed in, singing in chorus.

The nighttime shadows slowly crept away over the thatched cottages and the outlying fields. The morning sun shone on the town. Soon the wood-and-stone platform in the middle of the village square stood in clear view.

The platform looked sinister in the early morning light. The sun hit a wooden stake in the center of the platform. It glinted on the wood and twigs stacked high around the stake. And it sparkled over the townspeople who began to crowd the square, talking nervously among themselves.

"When she comin'?"

"I got chickens to feed. She had best come soon."

"The lobster will keep."

"Aye, so will the hens."

"Hush now. Here she comes!"

The townspeople turned to look at the wagon creeping toward them. The driver, his shoulders bent and his head down, whipped the plodding mule that dragged the wagon ever so slowly toward the platform.

No one paid any attention to the tired-looking driver or the exhausted mule. What caught each onlooker's eye was the passenger standing in the back of the wagon, her hands tied behind her and her head held high. She was a beautiful young woman with flowing, reddish brown hair.

Her name was Ida Black. She was an accused witch. And she was about to be burned at the stake.

Ida Black looked down at the curious onlookers, her neighbors in this small Maine town. She looked at the stake. She looked at a man standing at the platform's edge. When she saw him, she hissed.

The man, tall and broad and dressed all in black, took off his wide-brimmed hat. He was Colonel Jonathan Buck and he was a very important official in the town. He bowed to the woman in the wagon.

The wagon stopped. The crowd gasped in anticipation as Ida Black, her long skirt spotted with straw and dirt, was lifted up to the platform. She was tied to the stake.

The man in the wide-brimmed hat held a torch. He looked right at Ida Black's face.

She looked right back.

He bent down and lit the stack of wood at her feet with the torch. He spoke clearly and loudly for everyone to hear: "In the name of our Lord this year of 1691, I, the accuser, do solemnly light the torch of good and destroy another devil's witch forever!"

Whoosh went the flames as the sticks and twigs caught fire.

Soon the red flames danced at the woman's feet. They curled up higher and higher.

The smoke billowed out over the crowd of people, all of whom were talking at once.

Suddenly there was a screech. Ida Black's voice was heard from the flames.

"Jonathan Buck, hear me now and hear

me forever! You may have hurt me, but I will be avenged. I swear that you will burn in eternal punishment. And I will dance on your grave for all eternity!"

She burst into a hysterical laugh.

The crowd roared in response. Never had the townspeople heard a condemned prisoner speak so defiantly at the hour of death.

Colonel Buck ignored the ruckus. He threw more wood on the fire. The flames leaped skyward, and the roar of the inferno drowned out Ida Black's words.

Soon it was all over. Another accused witch had died.

The fishermen went back to their boats, the farmers returned to their fields, and the children went back to the schoolhouse down the road.

Indeed, everything went back to normal— except at Colonel Buck's house.

Although he had not shown it in the square, the colonel was frightened by Ida Black's terrible curse. It was he who had publicly accused her of being a witch. It was he who had told the townspeople that he had seen her perform evil spells deep in the woods. His testimony had convicted her. And he had lit the flame that took take her life.

And all along, he had been lying.

He had told the jury that he had seen Ida Black using magic to summon spirits and call upon the devil. He said that she had bewitched him, making him fall in love with her. But the colonel hadn't witnessed any of these terrible things.

The truth was that Colonel Buck had seen the widow Ida Black at the well one fine afternoon and, struck by her beauty, he had fallen in love with her on the spot.

He had courted Ida Black. He stole up to her cottage in the middle of the night and sang songs to her through the window. He brought her daisies from the roadside. He offered her venison and fish to stock her table. He gave her gold coins.

The colonel's courtship had worked. It wasn't long before Ida Black had fallen in love with him.

But when the time had come to marry, the colonel had a change of heart. Ambitious and mean, he thought he could better himself by marrying someone of his own social standing. He decided to marry the daughter of a fellow officer.

Ida Black was furious. She felt hurt and betrayed. She told the colonel that unless he changed his mind and married her, she would tell everyone about their secret romance. She would tell everyone that it was she he really loved.

The colonel saw his future as an officer disappear before his eyes. He had to silence Ida Black. He did it by lying, by falsely accusing her of being a witch.

And now she had cursed him!

It was too late to apologize. The colonel couldn't change anything he had done. Instead he spent the rest of his life trying to make up for his evil deed. He became a devoted husband and father. He gave generously to the poor. He went to church every Sunday.

But he could never forget what he had done to Ida Black. Nor could he ever forget her terrible curse.

When the colonel died, he had left strict instructions about his burial. He wanted his family to take great pains with his tombstone to ensure his eternal peace.

His family carried out his instructions to the letter. They used the purest marble for his tombstone. They hired an expert stonecutter.

They had the stone blessed by the church minister.

The funeral began. The colonel was buried, and the tombstone was put in place

One day passed, then another. It looked as though the colonel would be able to rest in peace.

Then something strange happened. Two days after the colonel was laid to rest, several rust-colored footprints appeared on the front of his tombstone. They turned to bright red, the color of blood.

Members of the colonel's family who had come to visit the grave stared at the tombstone in disbelief, then horror. The bloody footprints began to move back and forth, up and down, as if they were dancing—dancing on the colonel's grave!

The colonel's relatives didn't know what to do. They tried to wash off the footprints. They tried to sand the stone smooth. But no matter what they did, the blood-red footprints would reappear, moving back and forth on the surface of the stone.

Finally, the colonel's family decided to purchase a new tombstone. They chose a piece of thick black granite with a smooth and lustrous surface. They hired a stonecutter who had helped build European churches. They had the stone blessed not once, not twice, but three times.

The stone was put in place at the head of the colonel's grave. Family members looked on and held their breath.

For a moment or two, nothing happened. Then a swelling appeared on the granite. It moved and curled, finally taking the shape of a footprint, blood-red against the granite. Then another footprint appeared, and another.

And the footprints danced and danced as if they would never stop.

Frightened and bewildered, the colonel's relatives decided to destroy the tombstone completely. They broke it up into tiny pieces and threw them into the ocean. They raked the burial ground smooth and planted new grass seed. They prayed and prayed for the colonel's eternal peace.

But all their efforts were for nothing. No sooner had they stepped back from the burial plot than the ground began moving. Softly, breaking the soil, a series of footprints appeared, one at a time. Around and around the footprints danced on the newly seeded ground.

Ida Black had gotten her revenge.

She's still dancing, so it is said, on the colonel's grave. Dancing and dancing for eternity.

Messenger for a
Ghostly Love

PREMONITION. *One dictionary defines it as "a feeling of anticipation or anxiety over a future event." We see it at work when a fortune-teller reads a crystal ball, when a psychic predicts the future, or when we just "get the feeling" that something bad is going to happen or that we need to do something, without any concrete evidence to support that feeling.*

In the following story, a woman traveling in London in the early 1960s experiences a series of premonitions in the form of a voice inside her head. The voice urges her to take certain actions and eventually prompts her to strike up an amazing conversation with a total stranger. As it turns out, the premonitions have to do with a love that refuses to die. And to her astonishment, the woman who experienced them finds herself serving as love's messenger from the great beyond!

Mrs. Harrison woke up with a start. Her London hotel room was still dark. Cool air swept in through the window, swirling the drapes.

Mrs. Harrison rubbed her eyes. She looked at the clock on the night table. It was 7:05 A.M. She groaned softly. It was too early on a Sunday morning to be so wide awake.

But she felt a strange urgency to get up. She had the feeling that she had to get to church. Mrs. Harrison didn't know why. She was in London on vacation. And she wasn't much of a churchgoer, even back home in New Jersey.

"Hurry!" said a voice inside her head.

Mrs. Harrison sat up and shrugged her shoulders. "Oh, well," she said to herself. "It is Sunday, after all." She pulled back the covers and went into the bathroom.

Mrs. Harrison showered and combed her hair. She brushed her teeth. Then the voice inside her head spoke again.

"Church. To the church!" The voice sounded urgent.

Using her hand, Mrs. Harrison wiped the steam from her shower off the bathroom mirror. She began to put on some lipstick.

"The small church on the corner. Go now!" urged the voice.

Mrs. Harrison blinked. She looked different in the mirror. She no longer had streaked blond hair and brown eyes. The image in the mirror had gray hair pulled back in a bun, blue eyes, and a sly grin. Her skin was creased with fine wrinkles. For a brief moment Mrs. Harrison's reflection was that of an old woman.

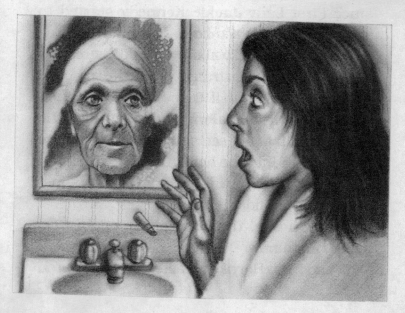

"Get going!" the voice in her head said. "Now!"

And then Mrs. Harrison was looking at herself, the self she knew, once more. She dropped her lipstick. She blinked again.

"Hurry! You can't be late!" the voice almost shouted inside her head.

Mrs. Harrison frowned. She wasn't scared, and that surprised her very much. All she felt was a sense of urgency. She had to get to the church—fast.

She dressed as quickly as she could. She put on her good blue suit and her new pillbox hat. Pillbox hats were all the rage that year, ever since First Lady Jackie Kennedy started to wear them. By eight o'clock, Mrs. Harrison was out of the hotel and walking down the street.

She felt a little strange, almost dizzy. Her feet were moving as if they had a life of their own, pushing her along the sidewalk. She hadn't remembered seeing a church when she first checked into the hotel. But there, right on the corner, was a small Victorian church—just like the voice said.

As if on cue, the voice spoke again. "Go inside. Right now!"

When Mrs. Harrison walked in, the church

was already crowded. She headed for an empty pew in the back, but the voice inside her head demanded, "No. Sit in the front."

Mrs. Harrison frowned but found herself walking down the aisle to the front of the church. The pews were all filled except for one seat, right next to an elderly man in a linen suit. He looked up and smiled at her as she sat down.

As she smiled back, she felt a jolt. Suddenly, Mrs. Harrison had a vision of a beautiful home, painted lemon-yellow with white shutters. It wasn't her house; she didn't know whose house it was.

Mrs. Harrison coughed. She smiled at the elderly man.

"Tell him," the voice inside her urged. "Tell him!"

Mrs. Harrison was determined to ignore the voice. She took out her hymnbook and began to sing with the rest of the congregation.

She looked over at the elderly man. He was having trouble finding the right page. Mrs. Harrison helped him.

Just as she turned back to her own book, she felt another jolt. This time she saw a wondrous garden filled with roses and tulips and big, fat bumblebees. The scene was so lush and beautiful that she gasped out loud.

"Tell him now!" insisted the voice inside her head.

Mrs. Harrison shook her head. She was getting nervous. She didn't know what was happening to her—or what she was supposed to say. Suddenly, she felt as if she had lost something. She put her hand on the lapel of her suit.

At that instant, something strange happened. Mrs. Harrison suddenly felt smaller and older. She felt frail. But she smiled as she touched her lapel. She felt a pin there, a favorite piece of jewelry. The pin sparkled with blue enamel. It bore the image of two dancing figures and a beautiful gold vase.

"Tell him!" the voice repeated.

Mrs. Harrison sat upright in the pew. She was no longer the small, frail woman she was a few moments ago. She touched her lapel again. There was no pin there.

She had never owned that piece of jewelry. In fact, she had never even seen a blue enamel pin with dancing figures.

"Tell him!" the voice urged once again.

No longer able to resist, but still not understanding what was happening, Mrs. Harrison finally turned to the elderly man next to her.

He was gone. The service was over and people were filing out of the church.

"Hurry! There's still time. In the back!" the voice inside her pleaded.

Mrs. Harrison jumped out of her seat. She pushed past the people mingling in the aisles. She approached the sunlit doorway.

There, silhouetted in the sun, was the elderly man.

"Excuse me!" she called to him.

Mrs. Harrison had no idea what she would say. But as it turned out, she had no trouble expressing herself at all. Everything began tumbling out: the lemon-yellow house, the lush garden, the elegant pin. She even told the elderly man about the voice inside her head.

The gentleman smiled as he listened. When Mrs. Harrison mentioned the pin, he nodded. "That was my wife's pin," he said softly. "It brought out the blue of her eyes." He brushed away a tear. "It was one of her favorite pieces of jewelry. It had belonged to her family for generations."

Now it was Mrs. Harrison's turn to listen. She stood there wide-eyed and amazed as the man spoke.

"You described our garden, yes, and our house." The elderly man bit his lip and shook his head. "My wife died last year," he said. "I miss her so."

The people in the congregation moved past them in the doorway. The sunlight continued to beat down. A bee buzzed overhead.

The elderly man sighed. "I can almost see her gray-brown hair, her blue eyes, her petite face."

"That was her!" Mrs. Harrison exclaimed. "I saw her reflection in the mirror this morning. I'm sure of it. She's the one who made me come here!"

"I'm sure she did. Oh, she could be a determined one when she set her mind to it." The elderly man chuckled. "I didn't want to go to church today either. My wife was the churchgoer, not I. But this morning, I felt this strange urgency to attend. Now I know why."

The last of the people had gone. The organ had stopped playing and the church was silent. Mrs. Harrison shook her head. "This is amazing. How can this be happening? I—I don't even believe in ghosts."

The elderly man nodded in agreement. "I know. But thanks to you, I know my beloved wife is waiting for me. I am at peace.

I will join her soon."

The elderly man smiled at Mrs. Harrison. He tipped his hat to her.

And then he was gone into the sunlit day.

Mrs. Harrison never saw the elderly man again. She never again heard his wife's urgent voice or saw the woman's reflection in the mirror. She never again dreamed about the beautiful house, the garden, or the blue enamel pin.

But she never forgot that Sunday in London more than thirty years ago—that fateful, sunny day when she played messenger for a ghostly love.

The Beauty and
the Vampire

*V*AMPIRE stories have been with us for centuries. Bram Stoker's classic novel Dracula, written in 1897, gives us a great deal of information about these creatures of the night.

Stoker's novel is based on a real-life prince, nicknamed Dracula, who lived in Transylvania, a part of Romania. This prince is said to have dabbled in the occult and learned the secrets of immortality. Everyone lived in fear of him. He tortured his enemies without mercy. He would chop off their heads and stick them on the fence around his castle. It is said that he survived for centuries as a living corpse by biting the necks of living humans and drinking their blood. Eventually his victims would die—and become vampires themselves!

Vampires, sometimes called the undead, are not without weaknesses. They cannot enter a house unless they know their victims. They cannot bear to be in the presence of a Christian cross, a vial of holy water, or a bulb of garlic. They cast no reflection and so they cannot be seen in a mirror. In addition, vampires can do their damage only at night. Before the sun rises, they must return to their coffins, where they wait until night falls again.

The only way to destroy a vampire is to seek out its coffin and plunge a wooden stake through the vampire's heart. Cutting off the head is another assurance that the vampire will not come back.

Vampire tales have sprung up in many parts of the world. The story you are about to read takes place in Russia hundreds of years ago.

———

Many centuries ago in old Russia, there lived a cruel, selfish count who was used to getting what he wanted.

If he wanted to eat dinner, he'd snap his fingers and tell his servants, "I want food, now!"

If he didn't like the cabbage or the roast fowl or the ale he was served, he'd fling everything off the table and yell, "This is disgusting! Bring me something I can eat or you'll all be whipped to an inch of your lives!"

If he didn't like the cut of his coat or the shine of his shoes, he'd throw everything into the fire and shout, "Bring me decent clothes immediately or be banished from my house!"

The count was never satisfied. His bed linen was always too scratchy. His desk was always too dusty. His food was always too bland. His chambers were always too cold.

Nothing was ever good enough for the count, and nothing went unpunished. Everyone in his household, from his servants to his secretaries, from his gardeners to his guards, lived in fear of his wrath.

But one spring day, the count spied a beautiful young peasant woman with long, flowing hair. He decided immediately that he must have her. Her name was Marushka, and the count made up his mind that he would marry her right away.

But Marushka was in love with Peter, a handsome, kind young man who lived on a farm outside town.

The count did not care. He sent his carriage to pick up Marushka and bring her to his castle. The townspeople turned and stared as the gold-trimmed carriage made its way down the cobblestone streets to Marushka's cottage.

Marushka had just come in from fetching water. She pulled aside the muslin curtain at her cottage window and saw the magnificent carriage stop in front of her door.

She turned and looked at her mother. "What is happening?" Marushka asked.

Her mother could only shrug. Then she went to answer the knock on the heavy front door. Marushka followed her.

When the door opened, the carriage driver pulled off his silver helmet and bowed. "The count demands that Marushka pack her belongings and come to him immediately," he announced. "He is to marry her by nightfall tonight."

"No!" Marushka cried. "I cannot!"

But she had no choice. Her mother helped her pack her one good dress, her comb and brush, and some ribbon into a cloth bag. She told her daughter it was an honor to be chosen as the count's bride. "You will have everything you ever wanted, my dear—jewels, clothes, a safe place to sleep. And you will be in a position to help us out as well."

Marushka knew her mother was right. She couldn't deny that it would be wonderful to give her family extra food, some gold coins, clothing—all the things they never had. But she also felt such pain that it was almost more than she could bear. "I must tell Peter, Mother," she said.

While the driver and the carriage waited outside, Marushka wrote Peter a note telling him what had happened. Then she wrote, "I will always love you, Peter, always." She pressed the note into her mother's hand and asked her to deliver it to him.

"Goodbye, dear Mother," Marushka said. Mother and daughter hugged each other tightly. Then Marushka went off to her new life. She had tears in her eyes, but she held her head high. She would do what she had to do.

And so Marushka and the count were married.

Five long years went by. Marushka was miserable. The count treated her like a prisoner. He kept her locked in her room and would not let her leave the house. He didn't let her mother visit. He didn't let her see any friends.

The count came to see her every day. "You are mine, my pet," he would remind her. "And no one else can have you. Only I can gaze upon your beauty." The count always locked the door behind him whenever he left her room.

Marushka learned to live with her loneliness. But it was very, very hard. She spent her days sewing collars and handkerchiefs, hoping to give them to Peter someday. She ate her dinner in silence, picking at her food. She spoke only when her tyrant of a husband roared a question at her. For hours she stared out her bedroom window, watching the swallows outside who seemed so free.

Finally, after so many years of misery, Marushka's suffering seemed to be nearing an end. The count was very old and, one month short of their sixth wedding anniversary, he took to his bed. He ordered Marushka to spend each day and night sitting in a high-backed chair by his side. She wore a veil to hide the faint glow in her cheeks. The only thought in her mind was that soon she would be free!

But as he drew his last breaths, the count clutched her hand. He pulled Marushka close to him and whispered in her ear so that only she could hear. "You had best not marry anyone else, my dear," he croaked. "For if you do, I will come back from the dead and haunt you forever!"

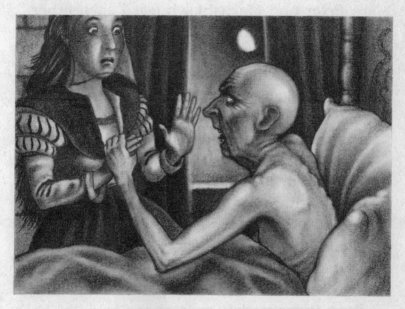

The count laughed and leaned back on his pillow. In the shadow of the flickering candlelight, he looked like the devil himself. Then he started to cough and soon he lay still. At last, the count was dead.

Now Marushka was not only beautiful, but she was also very sensible indeed. She did not believe in ghosts or curses. As soon as the count's body was placed in the family vault, she got on a horse and rode straight to Peter's farm. She would never return to the castle again.

Peter and Marushka hugged each other and cried with joy. They decided to marry as soon as possible.

As miserable as Marushka had been for those five long years with the count, she was now the happiest woman in all of Russia. She and Peter got ready for their wedding celebration. In two weeks, they were ready to invite all their friends and family to celebrate their marriage.

And what a celebration it was! The wedding party lasted three days and three nights. Everyone ate and danced and laughed, and there was no thought at all of the evil count. Those unhappy days were over.

But on the night the celebration ended, there was a terrible storm. The wind blew, the lightening tore through the sky, and the thunder roared in the heavens.

Caroom went the bedroom shutters as they

blew open. *Whoosh* went the curtains on the farmhouse windows. A picture in a frame fell to the floor. The candles dimmed and went out with a puff of smoke.

Most mysterious of all, a shadow came gliding through the night. It moved swiftly through the storm, coming closer and closer to the bedroom window.

The shadow was that of a man, an old man. As it sailed through Marushka's open window, the shadow took form and became flesh.

It was the evil count come back from the dead! He had become a vampire, thirsty for blood and revenge.

As Marushka lay sleeping, the count bit her neck and drank her blood.

When Marushka awoke the next morning, she didn't even remember the storm. But she felt very, very tired. She could not eat and she could barely move. She told Peter that she had slept badly because she had a bad dream in which the evil count kidnapped her and brought her back to his castle.

Peter, who had only a faint recollection of the wind and rain, was concerned about his new wife. He hoped she hadn't caught a cold from the cool air blowing through the windows during the storm. He made Marushka stay in bed. He brought her tea and combed her hair.

The next night, the same thing happened. While Marushka lay sleeping, the evil count visited her and drank her blood. She was even more pale and tired the next morning. She told Peter that once again she had dreamed about the count. This time, she said, he had appeared at her bedside in the middle of the night and told her that she would never be free of him.

Peter closed the drapes and urged Marushka to sleep. He hoped that a few hours' sleep would make his wife feel like herself again.

But the same thing happened the next night—and the night after that as well. Marushka grew paler and weaker, and she kept complaining about bad dreams. Alarmed by her condition, Peter called for the doctor. Peter told him about Marushka's nightmares. "It is so sad," Peter said, "that the count can continue to torment Marushka even after his death."

The doctor frowned when he saw the frail-looking Marushka lying in her bed. He was afraid she had caught pneumonia, but when he examined her, he found festering bite marks on her neck.

He made the sign of the cross and called Peter out into the hall. "I must talk to the constable right away," the doctor said. "I'll be back as soon as I can."

The doctor rushed to the police station and made his way to the chief constable's office. The chief was writing at his desk. He looked up, his smile quickly vanishing when he saw the doctor's face.

The doctor was pale. His hands were shaking. He leaned over the desk and looked the constable in the eye. He spoke slowly and deliberately. "We have a vampire in our midst," he said. "We must destroy him. Immediately."

The chief constable was skeptical. "Pooh. An old wives' tale."

"Not so!" the doctor insisted. "Listen to me. I saw the bite marks. I saw the victim's physical condition. I saw her look of horror when she glanced at the cross I wear around my neck. She has told me of her bad dreams, but I am afraid they are not dreams. She is visited every night by a vampire—the count she was once married to." His voice grew louder. "You must believe me, man. We have no time to lose!"

The chief constable sprang into action. He jumped up from his chair and began shouting out orders to his deputies. He told them to load their guns and collect some torches.

Then he and the doctor found a piece of good solid wood and fashioned it into a stake. They also sharpened a sword.

By the time the group was ready, the sun was starting to set. Led by the doctor and the chief constable, the men made their way to the vault that held the count's body.

Whatever daylight remained was gone when the vault door closed behind them. The lit torches cast grim shadows on the men's faces. The count's coffin lay on a marble platform in the middle of the room.

"Hurry!" the chief constable said. His men opened the coffin.

The count was lying inside. Suddenly his eyes popped open. His lips twisted into a smile, baring fang-like teeth. Then he began to rise up from where he lay.

It was true—the count was a vampire, a living corpse!

The count reached out to grab the constable's throat. But the constable was too fast for him. With not even a second to spare, he drove the stake through the count's heart.

The vampire grimaced, then screamed. Smoke poured out of his mouth. The doctor took the sword and chopped off the vampire's head. The smoke grew thicker.

Then all was silent, and suddenly the count's body disappeared in a cloud of smoke.

At that very moment back on the farm, Marushka felt a sensation on her neck. She touched the spot where the count had bit her—the marks were gone! She threw off her blankets and ran to look at herself in the mirror. The bloom had come back in her cheeks. "Peter," she cried, "I'm all right. I'm alive!"

Peter ran into the room. He took one look at his wife and gave a whoop of joy. He picked her up and danced her around the room.

They laughed and cried as if they never would stop. And the young beauty and her handsome husband lived together happily until the end of their days.

The Plantation Witch

WE all know that a ghost is the spirit of a dead person who visits the living. In some reports about ghosts, people claim they have seen shadowy apparitions that can glide through space and travel through walls. Other people report that they have encountered vengeful ghosts who are intent on haunting those who did them wrong when they were alive.

Mischievous ghosts have also been reported. These ghosts seem ready to vex and annoy anyone who gets in their way. Such ghosts are experts at nasty tricks such as slamming doors or moving objects or making scary, unearthly sounds.

These ghosts are called poltergeists, *a*

German word that means "knocking spirits." They cause havoc by making loud noises, hurling objects around a room, destroying property, creating strong winds—anything to make their presence known.

One such poltergeist visited a family in Tennessee in the late 1800s. But this ghost was slightly different from most of her kin. When she was alive, she had been a witch, and she carried the secrets of her witchcraft with her to the grave—and beyond.

In the backwoods of Tennessee, just over one hundred years ago, there lived a witch. She was a cruel and spiteful witch who would put a spell on anyone who dared wander near her cabin in the forest.

Everyone who lived in the surrounding towns knew about the witch, and they kept their distance. But the witch was very, very old, and one hot summer day she collapsed and died.

As chance would have it, the mean old witch died on the Bell family property. She'd been picking deadly nightshade on one of the

Bell plantation's vast fields.

But no one knew the wicked witch had died. For all anyone knew, she was still in her cabin deep in the woods, preparing spells and thinking up nasty tricks.

Time passed. The Bell plantation prospered. The cotton and tobacco fields were harvested and planted and harvested again.

One beautiful spring day, the Bell family children were playing hide-and-seek in a field far from their house. There were nine Bell children in all.

As one of the younger sisters ran to hide behind a tree, she tripped and fell to the ground. "Ow!" she shouted, gingerly patting her leg. Her brothers and sisters ran over to see if she was all right.

"I tripped on something," the girl said, pointing to an object a few feet away. Her oldest brother picked it up. It was a human jawbone.

"Yuck!" he said when he felt the dirty, rotting bone. He held it high, then threw it with all his might out into the field.

No one noticed that a tooth dropped out of the bone and flew through the air.

The other Bell children chased after the

bone and brought it back to the house. When their mother, Amy Bell, saw the jawbone with the missing tooth, she ordered the children to leave it in the shed out back where she would never have to set eyes on it.

Their father, John Bell, scratched his head and wondered about the jawbone. Who had died out in his field all alone?

The entire Bell family found out that night at dinner.

They heard a laugh first. It was a fierce cackle, one that sent shivers up the spine. Then the water pitcher on the table suddenly shattered, spilling water all over the tablecloth.

The Bells looked at each other in alarm. For a long moment, no one said a word. Then Amy Bell began wiping up the spilled water.

"Now children," she said with determination, "I don't know what that was, but I for one am not going to let it ruin dinner."

As she spoke, she picked up a forkful of food. She was about to put it into her mouth when her glass flew through the air and smashed against the wall. Once again there was a ghostly laugh.

Then, out of nowhere, a strong wind blew through the room. The Bell children screamed.

There was another menacing laugh. Then the spirit spoke.

"That's what you get for losing my tooth! And for tossing my bones in the shed!" Then the spirit pulled little Beth Bell's braids until she squealed. "That's what you get when you dare to cross me!" the spirit cackled. And for a brief moment, the family saw a swirl of black cape, long gray hair, and dark, scary eyes. It was the witch from the woods!

"I'll be back," the witch said before she disappeared from view. "Have no doubt about that."

Then all was quiet—but not for long. Day after day the uninvited guest made her presence known in hundreds of ways.

Patchwork quilts were pulled off beds in the middle of the night. Dolls and teddy bears were sneaked away and hidden. Fresh milk went sour in the cat's bowl.

The sitting room was flooded. The sewing room was covered in soot. Clothes were ripped, furniture was scratched, and mirrors were broken into hundreds of pieces.

The Bell family was very upset. No one knew when the witch would play one of her tricks. The children had trouble concentrating on their homework. Amy Bell had difficulty getting the chores done. No one in the family could sleep through the night. John Bell lay awake for hours trying to figure out what to do.

One night John Bell decided to sleep downstairs in the kitchen, hoping he might be able to confront the witch alone. He set up a bed near the fireplace. He took off his shirt, his pants, and his boots. Wearing only his warm woolen long johns, he snuggled into the bed.

Soon he was fast asleep. But in the middle of the night, he awoke with a start. In the glow from the fire, he saw his shirt and pants mysteriously floating up off the floor where he had dropped them. Not daring to breathe, he watched the scene in front of him and prayed he was only dreaming. With growing horror, he saw the shirt and pants take shape—as if someone were putting them on. He saw one sleeve fill out, then the other. He saw his pants pulled up over invisible legs.

Like a cat springing for a mouse, John Bell leaped out of bed. He grabbed the clothes and held them to his chest. Hugging the invisible body, he made his way toward the fire, hoping to push the clothes and its invisible wearer into the flames.

But all of a sudden, the shirt and pants became very, very heavy—too heavy to carry. And then the clothes began to smell. The stench was worse than the smell of old cheese or rotten eggs. It was the smell of the grave.

John Bell felt sick. The smell was overpowering him, and the weight of what he was carrying felt suffocating. He had no choice but to let go.

The shirt and pants fell to the floor. The witch soared out of the window, laughing all the while. "You'll have to do better than that if you're going to outfox me," she cackled. "Poor John Bell!"

He heard the echo of her laughter long after the witch had disappeared.

After that night, the witch took particular pleasure in torturing John Bell. She made him sick. She made his tongue swell to twice its size. She made his bones ache and his eyes burn.

John Bell couldn't eat, sleep, or work. And he most certainly couldn't laugh. He begged the witch to give him peace.

Finally, one night the witch spoke to him as he lay in his bed. "Have you had enough, John Bell?" she said. "I'll tell you what you can do to hasten my departure. Bury that jawbone of mine your little devils found in the field. Give me a decent burial. And be sure to find the tooth that fell out when they found the bone. The tooth has to be buried too!"

Then a gust of wind suddenly rushed through the room. Blankets flew off the bed and a vase crashed to the floor. "Find my tooth and bury me!" the witch screeched. Then all was calm again.

Early the next morning, John Bell went out to the shed. He pulled out boxes and cases and baskets, looking high and low for the jawbone.

He finally found the bone. But he still had to locate the witch's tooth.

He told his wife and children what the witch wanted. They formed a search party, spreading out over the plantation fields to cover as much ground as possible. But they might as well have been looking for a needle in a haystack. No one could find the tooth.

John Bell decided to bury the jawbone without the tooth. He desperately hoped that would satisfy the witch.

But it didn't work. Even after the jawbone was buried, the witch continued to torment the family and disrupt the household.

It wasn't long before John Bell's spirit was completely broken. He grew sicker and sicker, and at last he died. The family was heartbroken. John Bell was laid to rest in the family plot.

After her father's funeral, Beth Bell decided to take a walk. She walked and walked, thinking about her father and not noticing the distance she had covered. When she stopped to rest, she realized that she was out in a distant field, not far from the place where she and her brothers and sisters first found the awful jawbone. At that very moment, the sun came out from behind a cloud. Something sparkled on the ground and caught Beth's eye. There, at her feet, was the witch's tooth!

Beth picked up the tooth and ran back to the house. "I found the tooth! I found it!" she yelled.

And sure enough, as soon as the tooth was buried with the jawbone, peace returned to the Bell house. The tricks, the noises, the torment—all of it stopped. The witch seemed to have disappeared from the face of the earth.

But sometimes, late at night when the wind was particularly strong, a quilt would be pushed off a sleeping child. Or a toy would be whisked away and hidden on the top shelf of a closet.

And if one were to listen very carefully, a faint cackle could sometimes be heard just as the dawn broke through the night.

The Haunting of
the White House

*T*HE White House is perhaps the most famous place in Washington, D.C. It is here that American presidents live and do the work of governing the country.

Here are some interesting facts about the White House that you may not know:

- Although George Washington chose the eighteen acres on Pennsylvania Avenue as the site of the president's home, he never lived there. Construction of the mansion did not begin until 1792. President John Adams was the first occupant. He and his wife moved there in 1800.

- The original presidential mansion was burned by the British during the War of 1812 and had to be partially rebuilt.

- *Although today we know the president's home as the White House, it was not always referred to that way. President Theodore Roosevelt made the name official and used it on his stationery.*

And here's something else you may not know: A number of people claim they have seen Lincoln's ghost within the White House walls. Are these claims fact or fiction? Read on and make up your own mind. . . .

———————

Everyone knows that Abraham Lincoln was one of the greatest presidents in American history. He played a key role in freeing the slaves and led the North to victory in the bloody Civil War. Tragically, his life was cut short at Ford's Theatre in Washington, D.C., when he was assassinated by John Wilkes Booth.

But not everyone knows that ever since the assassination, a number of people have reported seeing Lincoln's ghost wandering through the White House. How do we explain such reports? Are they the product of overactive imaginations? Or did Lincoln have some unfinished business that caused his ghost to linger in the presidential mansion?

In the 1940s, Queen Wilhelmina of the Netherlands visited the White House as a guest of President Franklin D. Roosevelt. One night, so the story goes, she woke up with a start from a deep sleep. She heard a loud knocking at her bedroom door.

"Who is it?" she said.

There was no answer.

"Who's there?" she asked again.

All was quiet.

She threw open the door. There, standing in front of her, was a ghost—but not just any ghost. It was the ghost of Abraham Lincoln, clad in a top hat and heavy overcoat. His boots were splattered with mud. His beard was full and heavy.

Queen Wilhelmina looked directly into his dark brown eyes. His face had a serious, searching expression. Then he took off his hat and bowed. At that, the queen supposedly fainted and fell to the floor.

The next morning Wilhelmina couldn't wait to tell President Roosevelt what had happened. But the president merely smiled when he heard her tale. He knew all about Lincoln's ghost. In fact, his wife, First Lady Eleanor Roosevelt, had

told him she often heard Lincoln's footsteps. She said she sometimes felt his presence when she walked down the hall.

Queen Wilhelmina listened to President Roosevelt with astonishment. She didn't know what the dead president wanted—and neither did another visitor to the White House during those same World War II years.

Winston Churchill, the British prime minister, also encountered Abraham Lincoln's ghost. On his first visit to the White House, the prime minister stayed in the Lincoln Bedroom, where Lincoln himself had slept. Late in the night, Churchill heard knocking at the bedroom door. The prime minister simply pulled his pillow over his head to shut out the sound.

But the pounding continued.

With a sigh, Churchill got up and walked to the door.

"I'm coming!" he said impatiently.

Whatever was on the other side of the door ignored him. The pounding continued.

But as soon as Churchill opened the door, the knocking stopped. And the corridor was completely empty.

The event so unnerved the prime minister that without saying a word to anyone, he grabbed his robe, his spectacles, and his blanket and moved across the hall to sleep in another room.

Rumor has it that Sir Winston Churchill refused to stay in the Lincoln Bedroom ever again.

And then there's the report supposedly given by the practical, down-to-earth President Harry Truman.

After a particularly exhausting day, Truman was looking forward to getting a good night's sleep. To ensure his privacy, the president asked his guards not to disturb him for any reason.

He took a few sips of tea and read a few pages of his book. Before long, he was fast asleep.

And then the knocking began.

Instantly wide awake, the president jumped up and went to the door. He opened it.

No one was there.

The guards hadn't seen anyone. They hadn't heard anything.

But President Truman could hear something no one else could: footsteps echoing in the distance. Was it the ghost of Abraham Lincoln, making its way down the second-floor corridor? No one knows for sure.

Abraham Lincoln's ghost remains "alive"

and well even today. When Ronald Reagan was president, his daughter Maureen Reagan and her husband would visit the White House and stay in the Lincoln Bedroom. On one visit, something very strange happened.

Just before dawn, Maureen and her husband were awakened by a glowing red light. Shining like a halo, the light grew brighter and brighter, changing color from red to orange.

Eventually the bright light filled the room. Then at daybreak it suddenly disappeared altogether.

Oddly, Maureen and her husband were not bothered by the light. To them, it seemed as if the light was at home in the Lincoln Bedroom, as if Maureen and her husband were merely guests in someone else's room.

We can call these stories about Lincoln's ghost pure nonsense. There's no proof, we might argue, then shake our heads and walk away. But maybe Rex, Ronald and Nancy Reagan's dog, knew something we humans don't. He would spend hours barking and barking at the door of the Lincoln Bedroom.

And no matter how hard anyone tried to coax him, he never entered that room.

Houdini's Return

*E*VEN *with all the knowledge we have about our world and despite the amazing technology available to us, there are many things we don't yet understand. For example, we still don't know whether there is life after death. We don't know for sure whether there are such things as ghosts. And we don't know why some people can predict future events with such astonishing accuracy.*

In the beginning of this century, the quest to find answers to questions like these became a fad. People who believed that the spirits of the dead could communicate with the living called themselves spiritualists. *Those who could relay messages from the dead to the living were called* mediums.

Spiritualists and mediums held special meetings, called séances, to summon the spirits of the dead.

During a séance, a medium and several other people held hands in the dark and focused their thoughts on the dead person they wished to contact. Then they waited for a message or a sign from that spirit. The spirit might speak through the medium or write a message by guiding the medium's hand.

Harry Houdini, the famous magician and escape artist, could not believe the claims of spiritualists and mediums. But he was interested in trying to prove whether or not there was life after death. In the experiment he came up with, it would be his spirit which would try to make contact with the living.

He was the greatest escape artist that ever lived.

He was the magician who defied logic with his impossible tricks.

He was the celebrity his fans stood in line for hours to see.

And, if anyone could escape from death, it would be him.

His real name was Ehrich Weiss, but everyone knew him as Harry Houdini. Although he started his career performing card tricks, Houdini soon became famous for his ability to free himself from all kinds of restraining devices.

Before his spellbound audiences, Houdini would wiggle out of heavy leg irons locked up tight. He would slither out of locked handcuffs—at least ten pairs at a time! From escape-proof jail cells to crates nailed shut, from tightly twisted chains to airtight tanks filled with water, nothing could trap Houdini for long.

Houdini was also a master of publicity. He would arrange elaborate and dramatic stunts in order to promote his act. One of the most exciting stunts he performed was his real-life batman act. He put on a straitjacket, a tight-fitting white jacket with extra long sleeves that wrapped around his chest and back, binding his arms tightly. Then he had himself hung upside down from the beams of a tall building. Within minutes, he twisted himself out of

the jacket and climbed down to earth.

One of his most famous stunts was done in a tank full of water. He had the chains of a heavy anchor twisted around his body. Then he was locked in an airtight safe, which was lowered into a tank of water.

A sure death? Not for Houdini! Somehow he wiggled out of the heavy chain and anchor. Then he unlocked the safe and swam to the top of the tank to gulp some air—while his audience broke into thunderous applause.

But there was another side to Houdini as well. He was a rebel with a cause: exposing spiritualists, mediums, and fortune-tellers for the fakes he believed they were. Indeed, he spent a good portion of his act showing how their "messages from the other side" were faked.

Houdini discovered that so-called fortune-tellers claimed to predict the future, but in reality they paid spies to find out what a person wanted to hear. He found out that mediums used wind machines, trick photography, tape recorders, and even ventriloquism to convince people that spirits were actually making contact with them.

And yet, before he died on Halloween night in 1926, Houdini had given great thought to the possibility of his spirit somehow communicating with the living. No, he did not believe in mediums. But in the event there really was life after death, he would try to make contact with his friends to prove it.

Houdini told several close friends that after his death he would somehow communicate a different word to each of them. Perhaps to one friend he would tap out the word in Morse code. For another friend he might write down the word. For a third friend he might place an object in a room in such a way that the word would be clearly communicated. Together these words would spell out a message that would prove beyond a doubt that Houdini was alive in the great beyond.

After his death, no one heard anything from Houdini for a long time. None of his friends could claim that Houdini had communicated a particular word to them. But word had gotten out about Houdini's promise to try to communicate from beyond the grave, and a number of people waited for a sign from him.

Oddly enough, when Houdini's message was finally communicated, it came not to a friend, but to a spiritualist! A medium named Arthur Ford claimed to have received a message from Houdini himself. Ford said he "just knew" that the great magician had communicated with him, and he told the whole story to the public.

One night, Ford said, he was sound asleep in his bed. He woke up when he heard a persistent, irregular tapping on his bedpost.

Tap. Tap-tap. Tap-ta-tap-ta-tap.

Ford turned on the night-light and fumbled for his glasses. Then he felt his skin tingle. His breath quickened. There was a faint, pleasant scent in the air.

The tapping was definitely coming from the bedpost, but there was no one there. No mice, no roaming kitty, no maid checking the coals in the fireplace.

There was nothing but the noise on the polished wooden post.

Tap. Tap-tap. Tap-ta-tap-ta-tap.

Ford did not know Morse code. But he quickly wrote down the rhythm of the tapping. The next day, he had the message decoded by someone who knew Morse code.

The message was this: "I will love you for all time."

At first, no one believed Ford when he reported that he had received a message from

Houdini. After all, many mediums claimed to have made contact with the world-famous escape artist after his death.

But finally, Houdini's widow, Bess, had to agree that somehow Ford had indeed "conversed" with her dead husband. There was, she said, no other explanation.

For the message Ford received was none other than the inscription written on Bess's wedding band—*which she never took off.* The declaration of love was a romantic secret, the exact wording of which no one knew except Houdini and his devoted wife.

A Weird Tale of the Wild West

*G*EORGE Armstrong Custer graduated last in his class at the U.S. Military Academy. But during the Civil War, he showed a tremendous fighting spirit and became one of the youngest officers in the Union army. After the war, he went out west to fight the Indians. He was made lieutenant colonel, in charge of the U.S. Cavalry's Seventh Regiment.

As the white settlers claimed more and more land for themselves, the Indians began to band together to fight back. Near the Little Bighorn River, three courageous chiefs—Sitting Bull, Crazy Horse, and Gall—met to organize a plan to win back their land. The first step in that plan was ambushing Custer's regiment.

Custer knew about the meeting of the chiefs. But he didn't know that 2,500 Indians were ready to trap his 266 men. He was sure that his soldiers would surprise the Indians. Instead, it was the other way around.

The biggest massacre in the fight for western lands turned out to be the Battle at Little Bighorn, also known as Custer's Last Stand. This crushing defeat by the Indians is a well-known piece of U.S. history. What is less well known is that the battlefield itself is supposedly haunted. Spirits restlessly wander the scene of bloodshed where so many lives were lost.

———————

Dawn was finally breaking over Fort Abraham Lincoln in the Dakota Territory. But it was still misty and foggy, a damp, gray beginning to May 17, 1876.

The soldiers were busy getting dressed. They pulled on their boots and smoothed the creases in their blue uniforms.

Lieutenant Colonel George Armstrong Custer, the brave and tireless Indian fighter, had been up for hours. He checked his reflection in the tin hanging on the wall of his cabin. He smoothed down his blond hair. He took a deep breath and looked at Libby, his sweet, lovely wife.

Libby smiled as she handed her husband his coffee. But her dark eyes were full of worry.

Today, after all, was a momentous one. Her husband, one of the youngest high-ranking officers in the entire U.S. Cavalry, was about to lead the Seventh Regiment into battle. The outcome, so everyone believed, would be the biggest victory yet in the war against the Sioux Indians.

Custer planned a surprise attack on the Indians. Rifles at the ready, his men would storm the Sioux village on their swift horses. They were prepared to fight to the death in the valley below the stark mountain ridges along the Little Bighorn River.

Lieutenant Colonel Custer kissed his wife. "I'll be home just as soon as I can, my love," he said.

Libby followed her husband as he left the cabin. Wiping away a tear with the corner of her apron, she stood on her porch and watched the crowd by the fortress gate.

The cavalry band was playing. Dogs were

barking. Children were hugging their fathers. Some were crying. A few women and children waved small flags.

Libby sighed. There was nothing to do but get on with it. She joined the other wives, more than thirty of them, who stood watching and waiting, their hearts full of worry. She and the other wives bravely waved goodbye as Custer and his Seventh Regiment mounted their horses, lifted their hats in salute, and galloped out of the fort.

But as Libby waved, she had an ominous vision—one that made her heart stand still.

The fog had started to clear. As the sun pushed through, she saw her husband and his horse leave the ground. She saw him lead the entire regiment up into the sky. The men were dusty and bloody from battle. They were riding up to heaven.

At that moment, sure as she knew her own name, Libby was certain she had been given a glimpse of the future. She knew deep in her heart that she would never see her husband again.

There was no way Libby could warn Custer or his soldiers. They had already galloped away and would not return until their job was done.

When she tried to tell the other wives about her vision, they laughed at her or shrugged it away. After all, their men had already won several battles against the Indians. They were sure to win this one as well—especially because Custer had planned a surprise attack.

Forty days later, on June 25, 1876, Custer led his men to the Sioux village near the Little Bighorn River. But as it turned out, Custer's men were the ones who were surprised—not the Indians.

More than two thousand Sioux, Cheyenne, and Crow Indians had been waiting for Custer. They were prepared to save their land and their way of life at any cost. And they would show no mercy.

Custer's regiment was no match for the Indians. The fighting was fast and furious. Tomahawks sliced through the air. Rifles rang out and the shots echoed across the valley. Horses neighed in fear and soldiers cried out in pain and anger.

For the Seventh Regiment, the battle was hopeless. Custer ordered a retreat. His men needed no urging. Their very survival was at stake.

The soldiers whipped and kicked their

horses, frantically driving them across the Little Bighorn River. Those who had lost their mounts tried to cross on foot.

But the Indians were too quick and too strong.

Second Lieutenant Benjamin Hodgson was wounded by the Indians as he tried to cross the river. Another soldier was splashing through the water on his horse when he saw Hodgson limping along, trying desperately to reach the other side.

As arrows whizzed by and the battle raged on all sides, the soldier pushed his stirrup toward Hodgson. The second lieutenant grabbed it and held on for dear life. He was pulled along while bullets hit the water on either side of him.

As he was dragged through the water, Hodgson watched the Indians plunge into the river. He saw them reach for the scalps of his fellow soldiers. He saw the water turn red with blood.

Still Hodgson clung to that stirrup. At last, the horse reached the other side of the river and started up the bank. But it was too late. By the time the horse made it to the top of the bank, both its riders were dead. Hodgson still held the stirrup with his hands. His body lay lifeless. But his eyes were still open, and full of

the horror they had witnessed.

Not everyone died so tortuously as Second Lieutenant Hodgson, but die they did. Not one of Custer's men survived the Battle at Little Bighorn—but there are those who have seen their ghosts.

In fact, near the Sioux village, tourists have come face-to-face with ghostly soldiers from the Seventh Regiment.

One couple, sightseeing on their vacation, thought a movie was being filmed in the Indian village as they gazed down from the mountain ridge into the valley below. They say a dozen soldiers were sitting silently on their horses. Their shoulders were slumped. They looked tired, as if spent from battle. And their heads were covered with dried blood.

Later, however, when the couple returned to their hotel, they learned that there was no movie being filmed that day. And when they returned to the ridge to investigate, the soldiers had disappeared.

Then there's the account of a woman who saw three Indians on horseback near Little Bighorn. They approached within ten feet of her. One Indian had long braids. Another had elaborate feathers stuck in his hair. The third leaned forward on his horse to get a better look at her.

The woman rubbed her eyes in disbelief. When she looked again, the Indians were gone.

One man claimed that he actually heard Custer's ghost speak! He and his son had come to Little Bighorn for a vacation. They stood on the battlefield at the site of Custer's Last Stand. They were reading a guidebook when a man with long blond hair and wearing a wide-brimmed hat walked over to them.

The father hadn't seen the man coming. When he looked up from his guidebook, he saw a pair of blue eyes staring intently at him. The man was dressed in an old-fashioned cavalry uniform and had many medals pinned to his shirt. He asked the father, "Where's the Seventh?"

Confused, the father replied that he didn't know.

The soldier repeated, "Where's the Seventh?" And the father answered again that he didn't know.

Then suddenly the soldier disappeared, just like that.

The son pulled at his father's sleeve. "Dad, why are you talking to yourself? What's going on?"

The father looked down at him. His son had seen and heard nothing.

But the father knew what had happened. As hard as it was for him to believe, he had come face-to-face with the ghost of George Armstrong Custer.

But of all the ghosts that wander the bloody battlefield, the most disturbing is that of Second Lieutenant Hodgson. He has been seen holding on to that stirrup, his eyes filled with fear. The look in his eyes says more about the misery of war than do a thousand books.

Perhaps Hodgson and the other ghosts of Custer's Last Stand are destined to remain forever at Little Bighorn, reminding the living of the horror and cruelty of war.

The Rat Mummy

*F*OR most people, the word mummy is associated with the ancient Egyptians, whose civilization thrived thousands of years ago. The Egyptians developed ways of keeping bodies of the dead well preserved. Internal organs were removed and the body was soaked in a substance called resin, then wrapped in a linen bandage. These mummified bodies were sealed in painted coffins.

Bodies can also be mummified by nature. In fact, naturally preserved bodies have been found in the swampy bogs of Scandinavia.

But mummies are sometimes found much closer to home—and sometimes these mummies aren't human. That's the case in the next story, in which an ordinary woman doing ordinary housework makes an extraordinary discovery.

Quick! What do you think a ghost looks like? Maybe you imagine a tall, thin man wearing old-fashioned clothes. Maybe your idea of a ghost is a woman dressed in a flowing, wispy gown. Or maybe you think of the friendly sort of ghost, a little imp in a white sheet.

Whatever your image of a ghost, chances are that you imagine something in a human form.

But Aida Johnson had a very different experience with a ghost a few years back. The ghost she encountered was the four-legged kind.

It all began when Aida, her husband, and their children moved to a house in the Midwest.

The house was a typical suburban house with green siding and white shutters. There was a big tree in the front yard near the front porch, and that was all that distinguished the Johnsons' house from the other houses on the same street.

The inside of the house was typical too. There were three bedrooms, a den, and a dining room. The walls were white, the carpet gray.

At first glance, the kitchen also looked like any suburban kitchen. It was full of modern appliances, all white and chrome. There were calico curtains on the windows, and a round table and chairs for family breakfasts.

But in reality, the kitchen was the room that made this house different from all the other houses in the neighborhood.

One morning, Aida came downstairs to make the coffee. Yawning, she picked up the coffee pot and turned toward the sink. As she turned on the faucet, something made her jump. She hadn't heard a noise or seen any movement. But she had the definite feeling that she wasn't alone.

By the time her family came down for breakfast, Aida had put that feeling out of her mind. She had to get the kids ready for school and get herself ready for work. The rest of the day passed without incident.

However, the next morning Aida remembered that creepy feeling all too well. When she walked into the kitchen, she felt a chill. There were goose bumps on her arm. When she turned on the light, she thought she saw something move near the canisters on the counter.

Aida decided to scrub the kitchen clean from top to bottom. Maybe that would discourage the pest—whatever it was—from invading her kitchen. She got out a pail and filled it with warm, soapy water and, on her hands and knees, began to scour the kitchen floor.

Aida scrubbed the floor tiles hard, making wider and wider circles with her brush. She loved seeing the tile sparkle beneath her.

Suddenly, a tile popped out of its place on the floor. Startled, Aida leaned back out of its way.

At the same moment, a huge, gray rat jumped on her arm.

"Aaahhh!" Aida screamed. Flinging the scrub brush on the floor, she scrambled to her feet.

She jiggled her arm, but the rat only dug its claws into her skin. Then the rat ran up her arm.

"Help!" Aida yelled. The rat scurried up her arm to her shoulder. Suddenly it vanished!

Aida's husband came running into the kitchen. He saw her rubbing her arm.

"A rat," she stammered. "On my arm." She looked at her skin, expecting to see jagged claw marks left by the rat.

"I don't understand it," she said. "It disappeared—just like that."

Aida and her husband looked inside all the cupboards. They looked in the pantry. They looked under the stove and beside the refrigerator. There was no sign of the rat.

But when Aida walked over to the tile to glue it back down, she screamed again.

There, in the spot where the tile belonged, was a mummy—a rat mummy. Big, fat, and furry, it lay on its side, dead as anything could possibly be. The rat's body had been perfectly preserved in its dry tile coffin.

Aida's fast and furious scrubbing had unleashed the rat's trapped spirit. The tile, springing out of place, gave the spirit the chance it needed to be released. Using Aida's arm to travel on to the world beyond, the rat's spirit had made its final journey.

At last, the rat was at peace. As far as Aida was concerned, if she never saw a rat again in her life it would be too soon!

About the Author

With a degree in journalism from the School of Communication at Boston University, Karla Dougherty has been writing books for more than twenty years. She has also written for television and has had work published in magazines as well.

Karla says she was inspired to become a writer when she read Theodore White's *The Once and Future King*, which showed her what it's like to put yourself in someone else's shoes. Another of her favorite books is Kenneth Grahame's *Wind in the Willows*, which revealed to her that animals have their own exciting world. She is an avid fan of ghost stories because, she says, she's "still a big kid" herself!

Karla lives in New Jersey with her husband, D. J., and Bonnie, a West Highland terrier.